Contents

MEET TEAM DENNIS!

If you're reading this **boomic**, you just joined the COOLEST team in the WORLD!!

'Book' + 'comic', geddit?

Here are some new friends you're about to meet...and some villains you'll want to steer clear of!

DENNIS
BEANOTOWN'S PRANKMASTER-GENERAL!

GNASHER
DENNIS'S AWESOME DOG HAS FEARSOME TEETH THAT CAN SMASH CONCRETE!

MINNIE
DENNIS'S COUSIN, WHO KNOWS THAT SHE'S THE REAL LEADER OF THE TEAM!

KHADIJA RAAD
(SKETCH KHAD)

URBAN ARTIST SKETCH ALWAYS HAS HER DRAWING TABLET WITHIN REACH!

Welcome to...
BEANOTOWN!

Beanotown Library, Beanotown's tallest building. It has the most stories, you see!

Bash Street School, where all the coolest kids go.

This is where the Menace family lives. Menaces by name, Menaces by nature. At least that's what the neighbours say!

Chapter One

BEST SCHOOL DAY EVER?

ONLY A DAY AND A HALF OF SCHOOL TO GO. 129,600 SECONDS, 129,599, 129,598 ...

Dennis Menace isn't what you would call a big fan of school.

But, if you really want to know his favourite days at school, they are (in reverse order):

3. The Wednesday before the end of term

2. The Thursday before the end of term

And the winner of the Best Day At School Ever is . . . drum roll, please . . . you guessed it! The last day of term! **HURRAH**!

Today was the Thursday just before the end of term, so Dennis was in a pretty good mood. Not as good a mood as if it was the last day, but pretty good all the same.

And it was lunchtime already!

'Even the teachers have chilled out now,' he said to his friend Khadija. 'It's great! I wish every day was the last day of school.'

'Yeah,' she said. 'This morning I drew a picture of Miss Mistry riding down the stairs on Mr Throbb and she just laughed when she saw it! See?'

Khadija showed Dennis the picture she had drawn on her tablet. ——→

Stairs remind me of Dennis: they're always up to something!

WHEEEE!

OW! OW! OW!

'**Gnee-hee!**' chuckled Gnasher.

Gnasher is Dennis's dog and his best friend. He goes to school every day with Dennis, pretending to be his backpack.

Khadija is a bit of an art genius. Her friends call her *Sketch Khad* because she's always drawing. She draws on her jotters. She draws

on her hands. She draws on the ground with
a stick. Most often, she draws on

her tablet, which she carries
everywhere in her backpack.
Her backpack even has a built-
in battery so her tablet can
charge when she isn't using it.

Miss Mistry, Class 3C's
teacher, wasn't looking very
chilled-out when they got to class after lunch.
She was biting her nails.

'Come in and sit down, please,' she said,
anxiously. 'I have a problem.'

When the class had settled
down, Miss Mistry carried on. 'I've
made a bit of a boo-boo,' she said.
'I thought we had completed all

of our learning for this term, but it turns out that we haven't done our science module.'

The class was silent. Well, silent apart from the soft snoring sound Gnasher often made in class. Then Minnie farted and the class exploded into laughter.

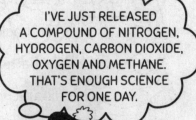

I'VE JUST RELEASED A COMPOUND OF NITROGEN, HYDROGEN, CARBON DIOXIDE, OXYGEN AND METHANE. THAT'S ENOUGH SCIENCE FOR ONE DAY.

'What's the big deal?' asked Dennis. 'I know loads of science. For instance, I know that gamma rays caused a radioactive pineapple to fall on Isaac Newton's head and that's how he discovered amnesia.'

Sir Isaac Newton discovers amnesia, as imagined by Dennis Menace.

BY JOVE, I'VE GOT IT! WHAT GOES UP... ER... OH BOTHER, NOW I'VE FORGOTTEN IT.

WE'LL BE BACK... IN 2025!

Miss Mistry groaned.

'I can't believe I've let this happen,' she said. 'I made a chart to track all the modules, and I thought I had ticked all the boxes.'

Teachers love making charts and ticking boxes. Have you noticed that? Almost as much as they love biscuits.

6

'This morning when I checked my chart,' said Miss Mistry, 'I noticed that the science module box wasn't ticked at all. Instead, there's a bogey smeared on it. I must have mistaken the nose-pick for a tick!'

Walter Brown, the class smarty-pants and Dennis's biggest enemy,

This is the bogey, if you hadn't worked it out – helpful Ed.

stood up and walked to the chart to get a closer look. Gnasher growled. He didn't like Walter either. Quite right, too.

'It's not a bogey, Miss,' said Walter. 'It's a drawing of a bogey, and we all know what that means – Khadija did it!'

And he pointed at Sketch, who stuck her
tongue out at him.

'Nice one, Sketch,' said Dennis,
appreciatively. 'I couldn't tell the difference
between your bogey
and one from
my own
collection!'

8

Miss Mistry sighed. 'There's nothing for it,' she said. 'I have no option. I can't send you all home for the holidays with an unticked box on my chart.'

I DON'T MIND IF YOU DO THAT. MY PARENTS WILL JUST THINK **YOU'RE** INCOMPETENT, AND I CAN LIVE WITH THAT.

Minnie is Dennis's cousin, and she will probably be PM of this country one day, and maybe even Supreme Leader of Unlimited Galaxies (SLUG).

Miss Mistry went over to her desk and picked up the phone. It was one of the old-fashioned kind with a cable to the wall even though there's no battery to charge.

9

'Does anyone know why Miss Mistry's phone has a cable?' asked Dennis, puzzled.

'So no-one steals it?' suggested Sketch.

The whole class held its breath, waiting to find out what Miss Mistry was going to do.

'Mrs Creecher?' she said into the receiver. 'Miss Mistry here. I'm just letting you know that tomorrow, Class 3C will be going on a school trip.'

SHE TRUSTS **US** ON A TRIP?!

'Yes, I am serious. Yes, out of the school.'

'No, I haven't lost my marbles. No, I'm not sure where we're going yet.'

'Yes, I know it's my career as a teacher I'm throwing away.'

Miss Mistry put the phone down.

'Well,' she said. 'You heard it. Tomorrow, we're going on a school trip!'

Miss Mistry stood at the front of the class.

'Okay,' she said. 'Let's brainstorm some ideas for where we can go. But it has to be science-related.'

RUBI'S SCIENCE-RELATED – HER DAD'S A PROFESSOR!

HA–HA! GOOD ONE, JEM!

'We should go to the moon!' said Dennis.

'The centre of the earth!' said Minnie.

'Those will cost billions of pounds,' said Miss Mistry. 'And we don't have time for a sponsored silence that long.'

'The pie factory!' cried Pie Face. Pie Face loves pies.

'What's scientific about that?' asked Miss Mistry.

'Well, I've done a lot of experiments with pies,' said Pie Face, 'and I've learned that my favourite is sprout and broccoli curry.'

'Well, that's *today's* favourite,' he added.

YUM! I'D BEST HAVE ANOTHER, JUST TO CONFIRM THE RESULT OF MY EXPERIMENT ... BURP!

'Miss, I texted my dad,' said Rubi. 'He says we can come to the Top Secret Research Station tomorrow.'

'PHEW!' said Miss Mistry, looking gratefully at Rubi.

'And he says he'll even try to rustle up a special scientific guest to give us the tour!'

'That's decided, then,' said Miss Mistry. 'Tomorrow we're going to the Top Secret Research Station!'

HOORAY!

On the way home, the gang were excited about their school trip.

'But who's the special guest gonna be?' demanded Minnie. 'Albert Einstein?'

'You doofus!' laughed Dennis. 'His name's not Albert, it's Frank – Frank Einstein!'

'Actually, Einstein's name is Albert, but he's dead!' said Rubi.

'Ada Lovelace?' asked Jem. 'She was the first computer programmer!'

'She's dead too,' said Rubi.

CRUMBS! SCIENCE SEEMS LIKE A DANGEROUS BUSINESS!

'What about that dude who grew potatoes on Mars?' asked Pie Face. 'I wouldn't mind a Mars potato and leek pie!'

'That was just a film, Pie Face!' laughed Minnie. 'I think . . .'

'Well, I hope it's Suzanne Pipette, the eminent French nuclear physicist,' said Rubi. 'She's my hero!'

They'd reached the gate at the end of the path that led to 51 Gasworks Road, where Dennis and Gnasher lived.

'I guess we'll find out tomorrow,' said Dennis. 'Come on, Gnasher!'

And the gang split, like the atoms in a nuclear reaction.

Only a bit less explosively.

Chapter Two

BUS TO THE FUTURE

A school trip doesn't count unless it meets the following conditions:

- You have to get on a bus

- You have to take a packed lunch

- There has to be a small chance that the number of kids who go on the trip is different to the number who come back (fewer kids is bad, but more is worse because you've kidnapped someone)

So, even though it was only a five-minute walk from the school to the Research Station, Miss Mistry had hired a bus.

Crumbs! Miss Mistry's bus looks bust! – Ed.

'All aboard,' she cried cheerily as Dennis and Gnasher wandered through the school gates the next morning. She ticked a box on the clipboard she was holding.

Dennis climbed onto the bus and nodded to the driver.

Jerry Khan the bus driver was weeping. A Bash Street School trip was the most dangerous assignment a bus driver could be given. He'd taped a rabbit's foot, a four-leaf clover, a horseshoe and a black cat to the windscreen for luck. The black cat wasn't happy. Gnasher growled at it.

PLEASE LET THERE NOT BE VOMITING. PLEASE LET THERE NOT BE VOMITING!

HI, JERRY! ER, ARE YOU OKAY?

Dennis shrugged and made his way to the back of the bus where the gang were tucking into their packed lunches already. Pie Face was a bit green. Dennis looked at Jem, inquiringly.

'Four bottles of Pink Cow Energy Drink already,' she said. That explained it.

Sketch was sitting on her knees facing the back window, drawing a picture with her finger in the condensation on the glass. It was of the mayor, and he wasn't being very mayorly.

VOTE MAYOR BROWN!

Cheeky! – Outraged Ed.

When everyone had gotten on the bus, Miss Mistry climbed aboard, ticking the last box on her sheet.

'Okay, Jerry,' she said. 'Let's get this show on the road!'

Jerry took a deep, steadying breath and started the engine.

'Let's sing a song!' cried Dennis, who then led the whole bus through 750 rousing choruses of the *Are We Nearly There Yet?* song.

It goes like this:

> ARE WE NEARLY THERE YET?
> ARE WE NEARLY THERE YET?
> ARE WE NEARLY THERE YET?
> ARE WE NEARLY THERE YET?
> ARE WE NEARLY THERE YET?
> ARE WE NEARLY THERE YET?
> ARE WE NEARLY THERE YET?

And so on.

Oh, and then there's the foot thumping bit.

You just stamp your feet in time to the words.

THUMPY·THUMPY THUMP·THUMP!

By the time the bus left the playground,

Jerry had shut his eyes and started to pray.

Amazingly, even with his eyes shut, he

managed to drive the bus to the Top Secret Research Station without serious incident. There were several almost-serious incidents, including the release of a herd of elephants from the zoo.

As they pulled into Bunsen Drive, where the Research Station was located, the singing finally stopped.

Jerry opened his eyes. Maybe this wasn't going to be as bad as he'd feared.

That's when the vomiting began.

Vomiting is contagious. You can catch it from the sound. You can catch it from the smell. You can catch it from seeing it. You can catch it from just thinking about . . .

Hang on! I need to make a run for the toilet! – The Ed.

It started in the front row, then the second row joined in and then it spread back along the bus like a tidal wave, which crashed against the rear window and washed all the way back to the front.

Jerry and Miss Mistry threw themselves against the windscreen and braced for the tsunami of vomit to hit them.

And then it stopped, just short of their feet. Miss Mistry opened the door and fled.

She was followed by
the squelching footsteps
of her pupils. Jerry sank
back into his seat. Even
though his bus
stank of vomit,
he felt somehow
that it could have been
a lot worse.

'Thank you!' he said, to
no one in particular.

And then the black cat
was sick on him.

SO MUCH FOR ME BEING LUCKY...

Beanotown's Top Secret Research
Station is where all of Beanotown's

best tech comes from. Rubi's dad, Professor Von Screwtop, runs the station, and he mucks about all day, trying to turn his crazy ideas into crazier inventions. Lots of the things he's invented are a bit useless.

Wow! I'll take two of each, please! Seagulls, sharks and elephants are the bane of my life ...

But he also invented batteries for cars that are charged up by passengers farting into the seat cushions. This was very popular with everyone except Mrs Pump, the owner of Beanotown's only petrol station, but she was able to turn it into a drive-through air-freshener shop. Cars that are fuelled by farts need a lot of air freshening.

He also invented three different kinds of super-growth serum, which can turn vegetables into power-crazed zombies intent on destroying the human race.*

Rubi led her classmates into the main laboratory, where a lady was waiting for them. She was wearing a lab coat and lots and lots of lipstick.

*Read *Attack of the Evil Veg* to see how that turned out.

'Hello, Class 3C of Bash Street School!' said the lady, in a strange, squeaky voice. 'I am Suzanne Pipette, the world-famous French nuclear physicist. My brilliant and very handsome colleague Wolfgang Von Screwtop asked me to come and speak to you all.'

'Dad, you're embarrassing me!' said Rubi, trying not to laugh.

'I'm sorry, little girl whose name I don't know because I haven't ever met you, I'm not your dad. My name is Suzanne!' said the professor.

'Your moustache is impressive, Suzanne,' said Minnie. 'You've got lipstick all over it.'

BUSTED!

The professor chuckled. 'Ah well, Ms Pipette was unfortunately a bit too busy to come today, so you're stuck with me.'

Rubi giggled. Her dad always made her laugh. He just pretended to be silly to make people feel comfortable, which is actually very clever and not silly at all.

'Now, Miss Mistry tells me you all have to do some science stuff, so who wants to learn about SLIME?'

The professor showed them how to make slime – his personal favourite is oil-slick black with silver glitter because it looks like the night sky.

Then he told them something interesting. 'Slime is an oobleck substance, which means the harder you hit it, the harder it is.'

So while you can slowly push your finger right into it with very little effort, if you jumped off a diving board and belly-flopped into a big tank of it, it would be almost as hard as concrete.'

Dennis made a mental note to try to make slime in the school swimming pool.

YOWCH! I THOUGHT IT WAS WATER!

Readers, meet Calamity James, the world's unluckiest boy – The Ed.

At last it was time for them to get into pairs and make their own slime!

Dennis and Sketch were paired up.

'I say we go **BIG** on this, Sketch,' said Dennis. 'You read out the recipe, but I'll misunderstand everything you say. So if the recipe says grams, I'll use kilograms, and if it says millilitres, I'll use litres. So our slime should be a thousand times better than everyone else's, right?'

IT'S TIME FOR SLIME!

'Sounds good to me,' said Sketch. 'And it's no one's fault because it's an accident!'

While Dennis mixed up his monster batch of slime in an empty dustbin he found at the back of the lab, he looked around. Walter and his sneaky mate Bertie were paired up and were looking to be mean as usual. Walter grabbed a handful of slime and tiptoed up behind Jem. Just as he was about to smear the slime into her hair, Dennis shouted.

The definition of a 'slimy snot-bag!'

LOOK OUT, JJ!

Walter was furious.

'Ooh! Now look what you've done!' he shouted. 'Luckily I have a spare pair of glasses in my briefcase.' And off he went with a sneer.

JJ fist-bumped Dennis.

'Thanks for the warning, man.'

'My slime is too thick!' wailed Minnie.

'I can't get my hands out of the bowl. Put some more water in, Pie Face.'

Pie Face had grabbed the fire hose and cranked it open. The flow was so powerful he was being thrown around the lab.

'HELP!' he cried. 'MAD HOSE!'

Sketch ran to the shelves at the side of the lab and grabbed the biggest book she could find. She took the book from the shelf and — stopping only to look at something she'd spotted hidden behind the book — dropped it on the hose. The hose was crushed, the water stopped, and Pie Face fell to the floor.

Miss Mistry helped the dripping-wet Pie Face to his feet.

'Maybe it's time for a tour of the Research Station, Professor?' she suggested.

'Ooh, yes,' said the professor. 'We can start in the laundry room! Follow me!'

The professor left the lab, followed by Miss Mistry and the rest of Class 3C . . . all except Dennis and Sketch, who were hiding behind their bench!

DO YOU THINK WE'LL GET A TOUR OF THE KITCHEN TOO?

Chapter Three

HOW NOT TO DO SCIENCE

'What is it?' asked Dennis, when they were alone in the lab. 'Why did you make me hide?'

'I found something,' said Sketch. 'Hidden behind the books on that shelf.'

They went over to the shelf and examined the dusty old bottles she'd found. They were very old and strange-shaped, and the names written on the labels didn't sound like any chemicals Dennis had ever heard of.

EMBARRASSIUM

MONKEY BURP

CLOWN SWEAT

STINKONIUM

'Embarrassium?' he wondered, taking a bottle from the shelf. There was some liquid inside, but the other bottles were all empty.

He strode over to the dustbin that was full of their slime mixture.

'If our slime is going to be truly legendary, we need to take it to the next level,' he said, pouring in the Embarrassium.

JUST A TINY LITTLE BIT FOR NOW... DON'T WANT TO TAKE ANY CHANCES! LOL!

The slime started to pulse, like it was breathing. Dennis was transfixed.

'Gnasher!' cried Sketch. She pulled the dog away from where he was licking up some spilled drops of Embarrassium.

The slime glowed like a bald man's sunburnt head, then started to bubble. The bubbles separated from the main slime and started to overflow from the dustbin into the room. Meanwhile, the main slime was still getting bigger!

'Gnasher!' cried Sketch again, dragging him away from the slime he was licking. He looked like he was slurping vinegar from a cactus.

'It's growing,' said Dennis.

'It's growing FAST!' said Sketch,
rummaging in her backpack for her tablet.
No way was she missing the chance to draw
something like this!

The slime had spread across the lab
and blocked their way out. Sketch scribbled

furiously on her tablet until she was satisfied, then tucked the tablet into her backpack so it would be ready when she needed it again.

'This is awesome!' she said. 'But how do we get out?'

Dennis was trying to take a picture of the slime with his phone. He hit the button.

The slime turned a darker shade of green and pulsed faster and harder. It stopped flowing aimlessly and started to flow towards them!

'What now?' cried Dennis.

'I think the flash from your phone made it angry!' said Sketch.

The blob slimed up and onto the bench and began to attack them. Dennis and Sketch batted it away by hitting it with science books, but the slime kept oozing onwards!

Sketch looked around for something – anything – she could use to drive the slime back with. That was when she saw the hose.

When she'd blocked the hose with the
book, no one had thought to turn the water off.
Now, the hose was bulging with gallons and
gallons of the stuff.

'It's gonna blow,' said Dennis. 'But maybe
that's exactly what we need! Gnasher, go get it!'

His faithful dog ran along the bench, leapt
over the slime, and sank his teeth into
the hose.

FWOOOOOSH!

The hose ERUPTED like a volcano, and water gushed into the lab.

The slime was swept away and down to a drain in the floor, while Dennis, Sketch and Gnasher sprinted their way out of the lab to safety.

'Great gnashing, Gnasher!' cried Sketch.

'Gnash!' said Gnasher.

'What just happened?' asked Sketch, when they were clear.

'I think we created a slime monster, then flushed it down the drain,' said Dennis.

'That's what I thought,' said Sketch. 'I just wanted a second opinion!'

IF THEY'D ASKED MY OPINION, NONE OF THIS WOULD HAVE HAPPENED!

Chapter Four

THE BLOB WHO LIVED

Once the fire engines arrived, it didn't take too long to empty the Research Station of water. In fact, it took longer to rescue everyone from the roof where Class 3C had gone to escape the rising flood.

'All your beautiful equipment, Dad,' cried Rubi, watching as scientific apparatus poured out of the research station's windows and landed in a heap on the ground. 'You've had some of it since I was a baby!'

'I know,' said the professor. 'What a load of old junk! I should have replaced it years ago!'

He turned to Miss Mistry and shook her by the hand.

YOU'RE NOT FURIOUS? YOU'RE NOT GOING TO SUE ME?

'Thank you,' he said. 'I could never have afforded to refurbish the lab and our living area but after this flood, the insurance company will pay for it all. This is the best day I've had in ages! I've already dug out my latest *Lab Geeks Mail Order Scientific Equipment Catalogue*!'

Miss Mistry didn't know what to say. If the professor was happy, then she couldn't really see that anyone had suffered because of Dennis and Sketch's little MISHAP. She got to tick her science module box, the professor got all-new lab equipment and the other pupils had had a great time. It's not every day you get rescued by the fire service.

She decided she ought to give out a little punishment though, because someone could have got hurt, even if no one did.

'Dennis and Khadija, during the holidays you can both complete a science project entitled *Why I Should Always Stay With the Group On School Trips.*'

While Miss Mistry went to see where Jerry had gone with the bus, Sketch showed her drawing of what had happened to Rubi, Jem, Minnie, Pie Face and Dennis.

'Is it really wearing glasses?' wondered Pie Face.

'They're Walter's,' said Dennis. 'Remember he lost them in the bin?'

'Why does it look angry?' asked Minnie.

'I don't know,' said Sketch, 'but when Dennis's camera flashed, it just sort of went into a fury, as though the light had physically hurt it or something.'

'That's right!' said Dennis. 'I took a photo, didn't I?'

He got out his phone and swiped through to his camera reel. The last picture was just a picture of the lab. There was no slime.

'That's weird!' said Sketch. 'It was definitely there. We didn't imagine it!'

'I feel a bit sad,' said Dennis. 'I – I mean, we – created that slime. It was alive and we had to destroy it, and now it's gone forever. It could have been an awesome pet!'

COME ON, BLOBBY, TIME FOR SQUELCHIES!

Sketch shook her head.

'Well, I hope we never see it again. We just flushed it down the drain. Hopefully it doesn't do any harm, wherever it's gone.'

Miss Mistry returned.

'After the vomiting incident, it seems Jerry has quit bus driving and gone to live in a cave on Duck Island,' she said. 'So at least it's not as bad as what happened to last year's driver.'

'Who drove us last year?' asked Pie Face.

'Ed Light,' said Rubi. 'He decided to escape from us on the last class trip by digging his way to Australia, remember?'

'That's right,' said Minnie. 'He sent us all a postcard from Woolloomooloo, didn't he?'

Hello kids!
I'm in Woolloomooloo, which is a very, very long way away from you!
Weather great!
Glad you're not here!

Ed Light

Miss Mistry's Class
Bash Street School
Beanotown
UK

'Well,' said Miss Mistry. 'If you can all make your own way home, then I guess that's it. Time to go home. You're all on . . .

HOLIDAY!!!'

Chapter Five

OUR SLIME HAS COME

The next morning, something was afoot in Beanotown.

> No, not that kind of foot. When you see 'afoot' in a book, it usually means there's a mystery that needs to be solved. – Helpful Ed.

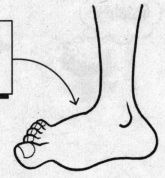

When Dennis and Gnasher went out, Gasworks Road was covered in glowing, green slime.

'This is a bit odd,' said Dennis, trying to walk normally through the goop. Gnasher plopped his way along behind him.

'Gnyuck!' said Gnasher, trying to pull his paws out of the goo. Gnasher didn't like getting slime in his coat. Mud, yes. Water, fine. But slime? Gno thanks!

58

When Dennis tried to skate into town to see if any other places had been covered in goop, he discovered that you can't skate on slime. But when he flipped his skateboard over, he found that you can surf on it!

In fact, slime-surfing was the newest craze in Beanotown. At the skatepark, kids were using skateboards and bodyboards to pull tricks on the halfpipe.

On Injury Hill, more kids were sliding downhill on dinner trays and skis. Rubi had fitted snow-skids to her chair so she could nail some moves.

'What a
brilliant start
to the holidays,'
said Dennis, when he
bumped into Sketch on
the corner of Bash Street
and Gasworks Road.

And he really did bump into
her. He was texting Minnie while he
was surfing, and Sketch was drawing on
her tablet while she rode a sledge.

OW!

'It is pretty cool,' said Sketch, 'but what if it's got something to do with the slime that we made yesterday?'

'So what?' said Dennis. 'Everyone's enjoying it, aren't they?'

'Not really,' said Sketch. 'Haven't you noticed that all the grown-ups are having massive panic attacks?'

It was true. Dennis had been so carried away with the fun he was having that he hadn't noticed the worried frowns and scared expressions on the faces of every grown-up he had passed.

WORRIED!

NERVOUS

HARD TO TELL –
HE ALWAYS LOOKS
LIKE THAT!

'People are all in a tizz because the *Beanotown Gazette* is reporting a strange, eerie green glow coming from Fartmoor,' Sketch said. 'The Gazette has started calling them the Northern Frights.'

Fartmoor is a high, boggy plain just outside Beanotown. The ground is very marshy and the weather unpredictable, so people tend not to go there much. Lots of supernatural things seem to happen on the moor too, such as UFO sightings and reports of horrid noises made by wild beasts that can't be identified.

'The mayor is furious because someone has smeared his town in slime, and Parky Bowles is livid because the statue of the Serious Man in the park has had its head knocked off and replaced by a giant cheese,' Sketch continued.

Dennis chuckled. 'I bet he looks gouda!'

'Sergeant Slipper is hot on the trail of someone who changed the street names in the posh part of town so they're a bit rude . . .'

Dennis giggled. 'Chestbutt Avenue!'

65

'. . . and the vicar is miffed because the slime has turned the church into the best bouncy castle in the country!'

Dennis grinned. 'So our slime is *pranking* the whole of Beanotown? That is awesome! I'm sort of proud!'

'It is kinda cool,' said Sketch, smiling, 'but we can't be sure it will stop at harmless pranking, can we? It didn't look like it was about to prank us when it turned nasty!'

'Anyway,' she went on, 'there's no way to know if it was actually the slime doing the pranking. Sergeant Slipper told me that not a single CCTV camera in Beanotown managed to catch any of the pranksters in the act!'

'As far as the police are concerned, they're looking for a team of messy pranksters and the slime trail is just one of the pranks, not evidence of who did it!'

'But don't you see?' cried Dennis. 'That's

what happened with my phone camera! I took a picture and it just didn't show up – it's GOT to be the slime!'

Sketch looked worried. 'BUT if Slipper is looking for the best team of pranksters in town, then that's . . . US!'

Sergeant Slipper's bedtime reading!

Dennis frowned. 'You're right. The slime is basically framing us for all its pranks! We could go to prison for hundreds of years, I bet.'

Sketch took out her tablet and looked at the picture she had drawn the day before in the lab. 'All I know is the slime we made yesterday wasn't big enough to coat a whole town in icky green gunge. Beanotown looks like a giant snail has slithered all over it!'

SLIME-ON COWELL!

'I want to find out more about this cool pranking slime,' said Dennis, taking out his phone. 'And I bet you ten of Gnasher's favourite sausages it'll be back out tonight to strike again!' Time for a groupchat!

Dennis: Anyone up for a bit of slime-hunting tonight?!

Rubi: Me!

Minnie: Me!

Pie Face: I'm against hunting on moral grounds.

Minnie: This isn't that kind of hunting. And it won't be on moral grounds, it'll be in the town centre.

Pie Face: Okay, I'll come. But I'm not blowing any trumpets, okay?

Dennis: Cool – meet up at the skatepark just after midnight.

Chapter Six

SCARES AT THE SKATEPARK

The skatepark is a spooky place at night. The floodlights cast dark shadows across the ramps and you can often hear the stray dogs who live there snuffling around for any morsels of food that the skaters had left behind that day.

The kids in Beanotown call the strays the Bash Street Pups. There are nine of them. Bones, Sniffy, Blotty, 'Enry, Peeps, Manfrid, Pug, Tubby and Wiggy. There's an old rubbish bin behind the halfpipe where they sleep.

Tonight, the trash can was firmly closed, and the kids tip-toed past so the pups wouldn't be woken.

When everyone had arrived, Dennis told them his plan.

'Let's go and find the slime monster,' he said.

'That's not a plan,' said Minnie. 'What do we do when we find it?'

'We figure that out when we've found it,' explained Dennis patiently. He'd never felt the need for a plan that had more than one step. When your plan worked out, you made up the next plan on the spot.

It had always worked for Dennis . . .

Apart from the time he was zip-lining from the roof of the swimming pool and ran out of cable.

And the time he trapped Ellis the escaped elephant in the alley next to Widl supermarket, and had to retreat.

And then there was the time he thought
he could reach 60 miles per hour on Injury Hill
if he and Gnasher both pedalled a lightweight
tandem. They almost did it, but in making the
tandem lightweight, Dennis had taken off
the brakes.

NEXT TIME, I'LL LEAVE
THE BRAKES ON!

there's a
gnext time?

But apart from those, and quite a few other
occasions, having only a tiny bit of a plan had
always worked for Dennis.

'I drew a map,' said Sketch, 'of all the places the slime left a trail last night.'

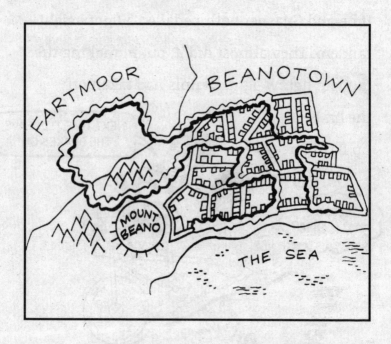

'So,' said Rubi, 'it looks like it **FART!** came from Fartmoor **PARP!** and went back **TOOT!** there when it was **FRRRP!** finished.'

'What?' said Minnie. 'I couldn't **THBRRRT!** hear you because you kept on farting.'

'I didn't fart! I **PUMP! BRAPPP! SKWEEEK!'** said Rubi, indignantly.

Pie Face pointed out of the skate park and up Bash Street.

'Er, guys? The **BLART!** is here!'

They looked. A giant blob of slime was trouser-trumpeting its way down Bash Street.

'Please destroy the school,' prayed Dennis. 'Please destroy the school!'

The slime tooted and parped its way past the school and kept coming towards them.

'**HIDE!**' hissed Rubi.

They scattered, hiding under the ramps and obstacles of the skate park, and watched (and listened) in horror as the slime drew near.

They could see that the slime wasn't one giant monster blob of slime, but was made up of thousands – millions – of little slimes who broke away from the main slime, making a noise just like a sneaky fart every single time, then re-joined it after inflicting some mischief on Beanotown. There was one bigger blob right in the centre that seemed to be controlling everything. It was wearing the

spectacles Walter had lost in Dennis's slime at the laboratory.

The giant blob butt-squeaked its way past the skatepark, while the little slimes peeled away and turned road signs so they pointed the wrong way, or teamed up to turn a car upside-down or move a garden shed on top of another.

Dennis was amazed. 'The slime is pranking the town, and at the same time it's making endless fart noises. It's like the Attack of the Fifty-Foot Whoopee Cushion!'

Minnie ran up the steps to the top of the halfpipe and aimed her phone at the departing, farting blob.

SAY 'CHEESE'!

'I've got to get a picture of this,' she said. The others stood and did the same. 'Quick!' said Rubi. 'Before it gets away! We have to get some evidence!' Their phones flashed as they tried to get a photo of the slime.

No luck. In every single picture, there was nothing to see. The slime just didn't show up in photographs.

Then, as they desperately snapped more and more quickly, their flashes raining artificial light on the slime, it paused. It drew itself up, then turned to look directly at them.

'Uh-oh!' said Dennis. 'Stop those flashes – they'll only make it angry!'

But it was too late! The slime throbbed and pulsed with fury. Dripping, grasping arms emerged from the main blob and stretched towards them.

'DUCK!' yelled Pie Face.

AND I THOUGHT IT WAS JUST ARMLESS FUN!

'**NO, DIVE!**' yelled Sketch, throwing herself off the platform and down the curving slope. The others did the same.

'Shh!' hissed Rubi. From where they had skidded to a halt at the bottom of the halfpipe, they could see the grasping, slimy hands clutching at the air where they had been standing just a second before.

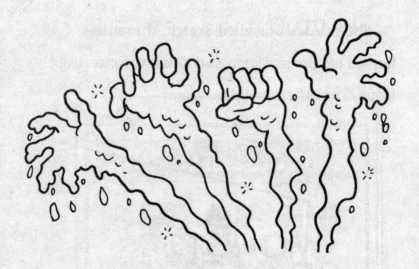

Finding nothing, the arms drew back until they were out of sight. The farting noises grew quieter and quieter.

'It looks like it's gone,' whispered Dennis. 'But to where?'

'Did you see it?' breathed Sketch. 'It was glowing like a lightbulb!'

Rubi stared at Sketch, then tapped quickly on her tablet.

She showed them the screen. It was the homepage of the *Beanotown Gazette*.

Beanotown Gazette

THE BIG BOG MONSTER OF DEEPEST FARTMOOR!

BEANOTOWN RESIDENTS REPORT THE RETURN OF THE STRANGE EERIE GLOW KNOWN AS THE NORTHERN FRIGHTS HIGH ON FARTMOOR. COULD THIS BE LINKED TO THE SLIMING OF THE TOWN BY AN UNKNOWN CREATURE?

'Minnie, Rubi and Pie Face,' said Dennis, making up the next step of his plan on the spot, 'you stay here and look out for the slime returning. If you see Sergeant Slipper, tell him what we know.'

'What about you?' asked Minnie.

'Me, Gnasher and Sketch are going up to Fartmoor,' said Dennis.

'That slime gets pretty nasty and if it keeps coming back to town, someone is going to get hurt. We made it, so it's our job to un-make it!'

AWOOOOOOOO!

Frightening Fartmoor! Even the Beanotown Tourist Board couldn't make this place seem welcoming...

Chapter Seven

FARTMOOR

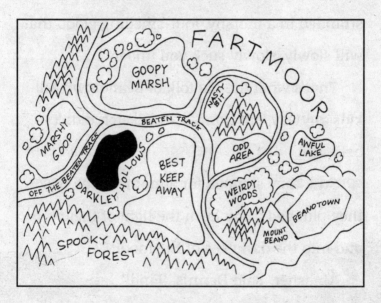

Fartmoor is only about half an hour's walk

from Beanotown, but it's uphill all the way.

Dennis, Sketch and Gnasher were out of breath

when they reached the edge of the moor.

Fartmoor is misty and mysterious. Ghosts and ghouls are said to lurk in its darkest hollows, and the rough paths through it can disappear from beneath your feet, leaving you stranded in a marshy, foul-smelling gloop that will slowly, slowly suck you under . . .

That's what the old folk of Beanotown tell kids anyway, but Dennis and Sketch didn't believe it.

Still, they stopped for a moment before they plunged away from the light of the town and into the darkness of the moor.

'Gnasher,' said Dennis. 'Find!'

Gnasher's nose twitched, as though it had been listening instead of his ears. The nose parked itself a centimetre above the ground and began to suck in air like a turbocharged hoover.

'Wait for it,' said Dennis.

Suddenly, Gnasher gave an excited little **'gnash'** and he was off, following his nose like a waterskier follows a speedboat.

'He's got the scent!' said Sketch.

Gnasher dashed up a small rise and vanished over the summit.

There was a 'yelp' and then nothing.
Dennis and Sketch reached the summit and
found themselves falling through space . . .

'OOF!' said Dennis when he landed two
metres below.

'WOOF!' said Sketch, when she landed on
top of Dennis.

WOOF!

'That's Gnasher's line,' said Dennis.

They dusted themselves down and got to their feet. It wasn't dark any longer. In fact, it was so bright that they had to shade their eyes.

'OMG!' said Sketch. She reached into her backpack for her tablet and stylus.

Dennis looked around, trying to make sense of what he could see. They were in a large, deep hollow – one of the biggest on the moor, Dennis guessed. By the strange green light, Dennis could see dozens, maybe hundreds of metal drums with a very scary symbol painted on them. Dennis knew what it meant: TOXIC. The drums were full of danger!

'Someone's dumping toxic waste in Fartmoor,' he said.

'Yep,' said Sketch. 'We shouldn't hang around long. Just let me draw it so we can show someone back home.'

'But the trail of our slime – or what we thought was our slime – leads here too,' said Dennis. 'So is the slime ours, or did it come from this waste dump?'

Sketch's sharp eyes picked out something

lying on the ground. She knelt down, picked it up and showed it to Dennis.

THESE ARE WALTER'S GLASSES!!

'Looks like the answer is . . . both!' she said. 'We can ask Rubi, but I think our slime has mixed with this toxic waste, and that's why it's grown so big.'

'AARGH!' moaned Dennis. 'Why can't science just be fun? Now it's going to ruin slime just when it got really cool!'

Sketch put her tablet in her backpack. 'I'm ready,' she said. 'Let's get out of here!'

'We have to find Gnasher,' said Dennis.

He heard a deep growling.

'There he is!' said Dennis.

'GRRRRRR!'

Gnasher was growling . . . at him!

'What is it, Gnasher?' asked Dennis, puzzled. Gnasher NEVER growled at him.

Gnasher took a step towards them, his mouth wet and drooling.

'It's the waste,' Dennis realised. 'Gnasher's been sniffing it in since we got to the moor – it's messing with his mind! We need to get him home!'

Dennis moved towards his best friend. 'Come on, Gnasher,' he pleaded. 'It's me, your pal, Dennis.'

DON'T YOU RECOGNISE ME?

Gnasher growled, louder this time. He took one more deliberate step towards Dennis . . . and disappeared!

'Where did he go?' cried Dennis. 'Help me find him!'

It was no good. There was no sign of Dennis's BFF. This was his worst nightmare.

'Oh no,' wailed Dennis. 'I've lost Gnasher.'

Chapter Eight

THE NORTHERN FRIGHTS

GNAAAAAAASH-ER!

'Where are yooooouuuu?' howled Dennis.

They hadn't played hide 'n' seek for years
and he was losing hope that Gnasher had
started a new game. There wasn't a single trace
of him – not even a pawprint.

Dennis blamed himself. He'd warned
Gnasher before about his bad habit of licking
anything gross that he found. He'd even
threatened him with a visit to the vet.

Vets, baths and dog leads are the three things Gnasher avoids at all costs.

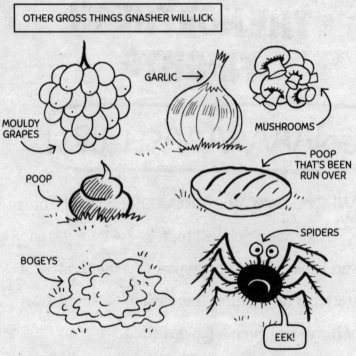

OTHER GROSS THINGS GNASHER WILL LICK

GARLIC

MUSHROOMS

MOULDY GRAPES

POOP

POOP THAT'S BEEN RUN OVER

BOGEYS

SPIDERS

EEK!

Sketch had already created a *Have YOU seen this dog?* poster on her tablet, but they'd need a printer, somewhere to pin it up and people to see it. None of these things were on Fartmoor.

HAVE **YOU** *SEEN THIS DOG?!*

The longer they waited, the farther away from safety Gnasher was.

Sketch nervously asked. 'Do you think Gnasher is maybe trapped in the bog?'

Dennis replied, 'Mum says Dad disappears away to the bog for ages, but *he* always returns.'

Sketch suggested they could try searching where the pools of slime seemed to be glowing the brightest.

It was a risky plan. Beanotown was covered in posters warning not to gaze at the Northern Frights on Fartmoor. The posters said they'd make your brain turn to slime. It sounded farfetched, but Dr Pfooflepfeffer, the mayor's favourite scientist, had done an interview about it in the *Beanotown Gazette*.

Despite this, they moved towards the glow, being careful not to tread upon any squishy parts. The marsh could easily suck them underneath the surface. **ON FARTMOOR NO ONE WOULD HEAR YOU CRY FOR HELP.**

It looked like they were playing a game of hop, skip and jump, nimbly avoiding splashing into the pools of slime. But the slime itself had other ideas . . .

Sketch jumped. 'Dennis, don't do that!'

'Don't do what?' asked Dennis, who was standing two paces in front of her.

A shiver ran down Sketch's spine as she replied. 'So, I guess it's not *your* slimy hand on my shoulder?!'

Dennis looked over and saw five large

green slimy fingers resting beside Sketch's collar. OMG!

He chose his next word carefully. 'RUN!'

Sketch leapt forward, tearing herself free from the slimy life form behind her. As she did

so, a massive, disgusting fart let rip behind them, first filling their ears and then, even worse, their nostrils! YEUCH-TASTIC.

They escaped into the stinky mist, running as fast as they could. The slimy figure was on their tails, and catching up fast. It was hopeless! Then, suddenly, the ground opened up beneath them and they were **falling . . .**

falling,

falling,

falling,

falling . . .

Chapter Nine

THE SECRET LAIR

Dennis found himself zooming down a large, shiny pipe that curved and twisted like the ultimate water slide. He could hear Sketch screaming just ahead of him. He started to feel a teensy bit guilty. Mum always said he didn't think far enough ahead. Come to think of it, Rubi said that too. And Minnie. Maybe – just maybe – they were right.

Dennis realised Sketch was screaming with laughter. His artist mate was loving it! She flipped around so she was sliding backwards.

Dennis looked SO funny. She'd heard about hair-raising experiences, but this was her first time witnessing one in real life. 'Dennis! You look like something being flushed down the loo!'

Dennis was going too fast to hear and returned a weak thumbs-up, which made Sketch giggle even more. Constant twists and turns made it feel like the most amazing flume you could ever imagine.

THEY BETTER NOT PUT THIS PIC ON THE COVER!

'This beats Beanotown Pleasure Pool,' yelled Sketch.

Once, Dennis's Dad had taken his toddler sister Bea on the flumes . . . without her nappy. She'd had an 'accident' at the top and the resulting mess had rocketed into the pool below, like a tor-poo-do.

It was as if a great white shark had gone for a dip, as disgusted swimmers clambered over each other to escape the stink. The whole pool had to be evacuated and was closed for a week.

HOW WAS I SUPPOSED TO KNOW YOU CAN GET SPECIAL NAPPIES FOR THIS SORT OF THING?

Bea wrote a 'letter of apology' (a potato-print picture of a poo that she'd added a large kiss to) and the Menaces were allowed back with a 'final warning'. Strangely, Dennis had always loved receiving one of those.

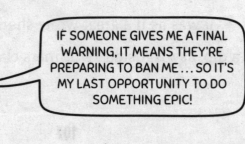

IF SOMEONE GIVES ME A FINAL WARNING, IT MEANS THEY'RE PREPARING TO BAN ME ... SO IT'S MY LAST OPPORTUNITY TO DO SOMETHING EPIC!

So he'd mixed mum's poshest bubble bath with the hair removal cream Dad used to defuzz his back, then poured the mixture into one of the 'groan-up only' hot tubs, on Dad Club Day. Talk about EPIC soapy bubbles! That was the end of flume rides for Dennis . . . and now this fearsome Fartmoor flume was ending too!

'OUCH!' Dennis had landed on something unusually hard and bony.

It was Sketch!

'OW! You doofus, Dennis!'

'Miss Mistry once described me as an unstoppable force!' said Dennis proudly. Miss Mistry had a way with words that allowed her to say something nice about even the most challenging pupils. 'Where are we? It smells worse than Bea's nappy bin!'

There was a dim trail of lights stretching into the distance of a long tunnel. They acted as tiny campfires for clouds of insects buzzing around them. *At least it's a sign of life*, thought Dennis, searching for a positive.

They'd landed in a skip full of leaky, stinky bin bags. Sketch insisted on trying to draw the epic route they'd taken as, for all they knew, it was maybe the only way back to Fartmoor.

Her map looked like a bowl of spaghetti – she'd captured every terribly twisting turn.

Dennis felt a bit queasy just looking at it.

When they scrambled out of the skip,
they spotted something printed on its side.

'**WOW**! Cool skull and crossbones!'
exclaimed Dennis.

I wonder what the 'W' means?
Any guesses, readers?

Sketch gasped, 'Not cool – it's even MORE
horrid. The skips's full of **TOXIC WASTE**!'

'Relax,' said Dennis. 'They sell sour sherbet
with that name in the shop where I get my
Beano comic.'

But he'd spoken too soon. He felt his toe

poking out from the bottom of his trainer . . . whatever it had touched at the bottom of the skip was acidic enough to have burned rubber! His foot then squelched into something soft and farty.

He peered down at a giant, slimy, pawprint. It faintly glowed in the dark. Dennis had seen Gnasher's dirty pawprints often enough to recognise them instantly. Gnasher's left paw had one toe missing, the result of an unfortunate incident with a velociraptor . . . but that's another story. The story here was the size – they were gigantic, and there was a trail of them, leading into the distance.

As they followed the trail, Dennis started to worry. What had happened to his best pal? Had he grown to a giant size from eating

toxic slime, or was it just his paws that had grown massive? His own foot began to itch, right where the toxic slime had seeped in. He shivered. What if his feet inflated? Could he still get cool trainers the size of clown shoes?!

His worries were rudely interrupted by two voices, overlapping in argument. Squabbles never sound good. In dark tunnels, they sound SCARY! Dennis recognised the voices. It was Mayor Wilbur Brown, complaining to the expert scientist, Dr Pfooflepfeffer. She was speaking extraordinarily loudly!

They crept along towards the voices. The tunnel widened into a large room, packed with bright lights, screens and buttons. The first thing they saw was Dr P. standing proudly in the middle of the large chamber, and she was GINORMOUS!

'Look, Sketch! She's grown massive! That explains the pawprints. Gnasher must be that big too. We're in the land of the giants!' whispered Dennis.

CAN YOU HEAR
ME UP THERE,
PFOOFLEPFEFFER?

But as they tuned into what Wilbur was
saying and located him, they saw he was still
only regular size. What was going on?!

'Yes, of course I could shut the energy plant
down, but that would cost me a fortune. Isn't
there another option? Find one! That's what I
pay you for!'

He continued to moan. 'You promised cheap bio energy, using Screwtop's Secret Slime Formula. But what I've got smells like cheap B.O. energy – the stench of a million hairy armpits!'

Dr Pfooflepfeffer didn't seem fazed, but then again, she was nearly ten metres tall. 'Relax, Willy. The nasty niff is essential. It's what keeps snoopers away. Even an ogre wouldn't live on Fartmoor nowadays.'

Wilbur bit back, 'But Beanotown is obsessed with 'Slimezilla'. It won't be long until they make the link with me. The Pranking Slime Monster, they're calling it. It's running riot.'

'That's just a teething problem,' she replied.

'It'll be a teething problem if it eats someone!' ranted Wilbur.

Dr P. just grinned back. 'We needed a new distraction. The story we leaked to the *Gazette* about the Bog Monster was wearing a bit thin.'

Beanotown Gazette

MAYOR CLAIMS AWFUL SMELL COMING FROM BOG
(DOESN'T SAY IF IT'S HIS BOG)

Wibur slapped his hand to his forehead in frustration. **SMACK!**

Dr Pfooflepfeffer laughed gently. 'Relax. We won't get the blame. That idiot Sergeant Slipper is convinced it's all down to that horrible Dennis kid and his friends.'

'Harumph! Speaking of lame stories, it was YOU who promised Screwtop's energy-generating experiments would make me squillions of pounds.'

For the first time, Pfooflepfeffer looked annoyed. 'But I never told you to hire a team of ninjas to steal them, then build a secret power plant beneath Fartmoor.'

Wilbur smirked. 'Yes, but how else could I have raked it in by selling dirty energy to thousands of Beanotown bozos who think it's clean? That's the genius part of the project. I do wish I could grow a moustache to twirl at moments like this.'

Dennis knew Dad had already wired their

own electricity into Wilbur's supply next door. They also piggybacked onto his Wi-Fi to play Fartnite. He felt like popping Wilbur's smugness, but Sketch shot him a look that said, 'Just zip it!'

Dennis had started to get the same sinking feeling he always got when he realised he was about to get into trouble. He didn't mind taking the blame when he caused trouble on purpose, but it was a sickener when you got into trouble by accident.

His nose had started to tingle too. His Menace sense, passed down through generations, had been activated. Something weird was going down. Wilbur had fallen silent and was standing stock still.

'Has the cat got your tongue?' asked the smug Dr Pfooflepfeffer.

> Mrs Creecher, the headteacher at Bash Street School, often used that phrase. Older pupils said it originated from the ancient Viking school punishment of persistently talkative pupils having their tongues snipped off and fed to the janitor's cat. It had been rumoured Creecher favoured bringing it back! – The Ed.

Wilbur didn't reply. Dr Pfooflepfeffer started to fade from view then disappeared completely.

'Where did she go?' asked Dennis.

'Ooh!' said Sketch. 'She was just a hologram! Her 5G connection probably dropped out. It's hard to get a signal up here on Fartmoor.'

'Hologram, shmologram!' said Dennis. 'I thought she was actually humungous!'

Dennis was disappointed. He'd been pretty excited about potentially being in the land of the giants. Wilbur had started to move again. In fact, he was quivering like a jelly.

GNAAASSSSSSSH!

GNAAAAAAAAAAAASSSSH!

The growl was so loud, Dennis felt the air around him vibrate. He looked past Wilbur to see it was Gnasher who was approaching, only he'd grown as big as an elephant!

'Dr Pfooflepfeffer's hologram tech is amazeballs,' he said to Sketch, who was copying the scene in front of them onto her tablet.

But before Dennis could even say, 'a doggy that size could swallow Wilbur in one bite,' Gnasher lurched forward and noisily slurped a frantically waving Wilbur into his mouth. The once-proud Mayor screamed pathetically (well, you would too in that situation).

SHRIEK! I WANT MY MUMMY!

'Gnasher's never tried posh food before,' said Dennis.

Sketch stopped drawing in horror. 'Eating the Mayor is actually worse than slime. No one's ever been able to stomach his snooty attitude! YEUCH!'

Gnasher heard this and looked up. Dennis thought he was about to join Wilbur as dog food, but Gnasher could never completely forget his pedigree chum. He spat out Wilbur, leaving him sprawled, dazed and confused upon the floor, and then, in a single joyous bound, was back with his friends.

A shamefaced, slimy Wilbur struggled to his feet, only to immediately slip over again after losing his footing in the pile of gloop surrounding him. All the scene needed was a drumroll followed by a cymbal crash!

Wilbur picked himself up then shook himself like a wet dog, removing some gloop from his expensive designer suit. He started to raise an angry fist, but before he could even begin to shake it, another low growl saw him bolt between Gnasher's legs and dash straight past Dennis and Sketch.

Gnasher sloppily licked his pals, eager to remove the bad taste of Wilbur from his mouth. His tongue was like a soggy pink bath towel. URGH.

'Gee thanks, Gnasher! I knew we had nothing to worry about,' said Dennis.

'Apart from him STILL being the size of an elephant,' laughed Sketch. 'I think swallowing some slime made him grow . . . he got so big,

URGH!
I LOVE YOU
TOO, BUDDY!

he sank straight through the swamp. The slime
just chased us into the hole Gnasher made.'

Dennis looked confused. 'So Gnasher's
growing just like our slime pet did? Is he going
to make those epic farty sounds too?'

'Yes, it's clear now. The slime produces terrible wind that makes it change shape and grow – the only way it can control it is by constantly pumping. It's like letting air in and out of a party balloon. Gnasher's got wind after eating slime. He just needs to fart to let it go . . .'

'But why did he growl at US?' asked Dennis.

'I think he knew something bad was happening to him, and he wanted us to leave before it happened to us too.'

Chapter Ten

THE FATHER OF ALL INVENTIONS

Gnasher took a step in the direction he had come from, then paused.

'**EEK**! If Gnasher needs a giant doggie-do, we're both history!'

The pair synchronised a step backwards. The humungous hound bounded away, his giant legs propelling him so quickly that Dennis and Sketch couldn't have hoped to keep up . . .

But their close encounter had inspired Sketch to scribble some rough doggy doodles

127

onto her tablet. She chewed her lip, as if she was trying to make sense of something.

Dennis noticed Sketch was drawing his dog's butt. He'd recently visited the new Beanotown Urban Museum of Modern Art (BUMoMA), where the star exhibit was a slice of toast, so maybe Sketch had just attempted her own masterpiece? She stopped drawing to ask, 'How many times a day does Gnasher normally pump?'

'Never, but only cos we sneak a special fart-repellent tablet in with his breakfast sausages. Before that, he farted like a trooper. A pooper trooper!' giggled Dennis.

'So Gnasher's now the only pooch in the entire world who never farts?'

'Yep. Gran imported the tablets from the

USA. One a day keeps the trumps away. Mum

sneaks them in Dad's bedtime cocoa too. It's the

only way she can get a good night's sleep . . .'

Before they'd gone far, Dennis spotted a

golf kart. There was a sticker on its bonnet:

PROPERTY OF
BEANOTOWN GOLF CLUB
DO NOT REMOVE

He shook his head. 'What a cheapskate. Stealing a golf buggy suits Wilbur to a tee.'

The pair jumped in and Sketch hit the accelerator. They caught up with Gnasher, who was balancing on his hind legs, stretching up to lick what appeared to be a hatch on the tunnel's ceiling. Sketch braked and they skidded to a halt, almost losing control due to the slimy pawprints everywhere.

Gnasher bent down and nudged a very dizzy Dennis to clamber onto his nose. He then raised his mate up to the hatch. He wanted him to open it! Dennis struggled with the hatch but couldn't budge it. He paused and yelled to Sketch.

'What if this lets the Fartmoor Bog flood in? Can you check your map?' His feet started

HURRY! WHO NOSE HOW LONG I CAN STAY ON MY FEET?!

to skid wildly on the snot streaming from Gnasher's nostrils.

'Be careful,' yelled Sketch, as she opened her map on her tablet. 'I think you're about to make Gnasher . . .'

GNATCHOOO!

The stupendous sneeze propelled Dennis straight through the hatch, his head bashing into it with a DING, followed quickly by a dull DONG as it slammed shut behind him.

A dazed Dennis came around in a brilliantly bright white space. He was lying crumpled, like a used, extremely snotty, tissue, next to a concerned-looking Professor Von Screwtop. Staring down at him was Rubi!

IT'S SNOT GOOD TO SEE YOU!

'What do you think you're doing, Dennis?' she demanded.

'We were chilling, doing a bit of yoga when you popped up. You could have brained my dad!'

'I'm fine, my dear,' interrupted the professor. 'But how is my young spiky-haired friend doing?'

Dennis was feeling a lot better. Having super-smart Rubi and her dad on the case was exactly what they needed.

The prof admitted he'd always wondered where that odd hatch went but had never got round to trying to open it. Suddenly, it started to make a weird metallic tapping noise. Rubi looked at Dennis, confused at first, before she realised it was a message being sent using

Morse code. Rubi translated the taps, letter by letter, word by word . . .

'Let – me – in – doofus . . . um, sorry, maybe that's wrong. Maybe it means "Dennis"? Who, or what, is doing that?'

'**OOPS!** I almost forgot, Sketch is still stuck down there – and Gnasher too!'

Rubi shook her head at Dennis for forgetting his mates, then lifted the hatch. Sketch popped through.

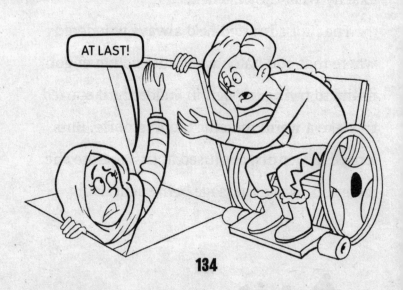

AT LAST!

'You were right the first time,' she said. 'I was calling him doofus!'

Gnasher squeezed his nose through and sniffed noisily. It looked like a giant black olive poking out from the floor! This brought back some bad memories for Professor Von Screwtop – about the army of evil veg that had attacked his lab a while back. He knew olives were actually fruit, but so were those terrifying tomatoes he'd faced!

There was no way Gnasher could join them, at least not without wrecking the entire lab! Dennis and Sketch quickly explained their theory about why Gnasher was supersized and how they'd discovered Wilbur's fiendish scheme to rip people off, with environmental disaster as a slimy side effect.

When they mentioned Dr Pfooflepfeffer, the professor let out a loud sigh. He explained how he'd been working with her on a revolutionary way to generate clean, environmentally sound gas and electricity. The technology relied on combining solar-radiated slime with an invention the professor had pioneered: Fission Chips.

'The power produced would be clean, cheap and plentiful. But I just couldn't get it to work properly. There were too many side effects.'

'The worst was the production of stinky toxic slime. The yucky stuff you can see on

Fartmoor. I fed some to my Venus flytrap and it grew bigger than me and just wouldn't stop burping. One of the giant bugs that infested the town gobbled it up before I could investigate further . . . but I was worried enough to stop my research.'

Rubi chipped in. 'I remember how Pfooflepfeffer begged you to continue because there was so much money to be made. Why didn't she just continue alone?' asked Rubi.

'Simple. I didn't share my chips!' answered the prof. 'Dr P. knew how to use light to activate slime, but she couldn't make Fission Chips. I hid them in my lab and refused to take any of her calls. I only follow her on ProfBook because I didn't want to seem rude by unfriending her . . .'

'Dad, where *exactly* did you hide the Fission Chips?' asked Rubi nervously.

'I preserved them in a jar, which I cunningly disguised with the name of a completely made-up chemical that I invented,' he giggled. 'No serious scientist would dream of picking it up! Sometimes, I am indeed a genius.'

Rubi asked what the hilarious name her dad had invented was. The name that would mean no one would discover his Fission Chips?

'I called it . . . Embarrassium! Genius, no?'

'**UH-OH!**' said Dennis.

Chapter Eleven

DON'T PRESS IT, DENNIS!

They took turns to balance on Gnasher's giant snotty nose, in order to be lowered safely back down to the tunnel below.

Professor Von Screwtop had always wanted a dog. He'd been fired by several labs for releasing lab animals the other scientists wished to test upon. He trusted his science so much, he tested everything on himself anyway! Animals loved him. Gnasher was no exception, and he snuzzled into his lab coat.

The prof was fascinated. Gnasher was smarter than the average human, make no mistake. An interesting fact not a lot of people know about Gnasher is that every Halloween, for one day only, he's able to speak, human-style, in whichever language he chooses.

Dennis obviously knew this. He also realised Gnasher could easily understand anything he said at any time. But this wasn't a secret Dennis shared, not even with his mates.

140

He caught Gnasher's eye.

'Gnash, have you spotted anything scientifically important down here? Not including any sausages.'

Gnasher nodded, then dashed farther ahead down the tunnel. They piled into the golf buggy to catch up. When they did, a jaw-dropping sight awaited them . . .

They'd arrived at a large chamber, carved into the rock. In the centre was something that looked like a giant fountain, covered by a smooth clear dome. It looked like the sort of contraption you might see at a posh wedding, that would keep melted chocolate flowing to let you to dip in strawberries, marshmallows, bogies . . . UH? Well, anything tastes good after being dipped into a chocolate fountain.

Except, it wasn't chocolate in this one, but slime. Green, gloopy, squelchy, smelly slime. It cascaded, splashed and . . . crackled! But, most unusually, it farted! Continuously. It sounded . . . hilarious!

There were electronic sensors hanging just above the slime. As the slime bubbled up and touched them, a faint sizzling sound could be heard. The slime was reacting, and generating small amounts of electricity. As the green slime released the energy it contained, it turned brown and sank to the bottom. This brown sludge was then pumped out of the tank and blasted skywards through a hole in the roof . . . straight out into the ominous bogs of Fartmoor!

At the same time, gas from the farts was being extracted by a large suction fan.

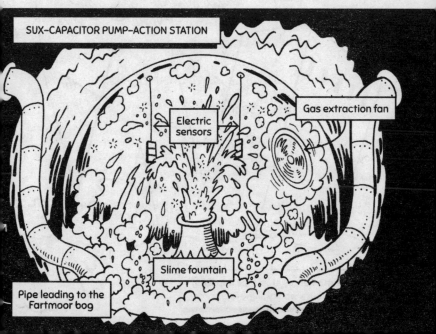

SUX-CAPACITOR PUMP-ACTION STATION

Electric sensors

Gas extraction fan

Slime fountain

Pipe leading to the Fartmoor bog

'Look at that!' exclaimed the professor.
'My SUX-CAPACITOR PUMP-ACTION STATION!
I invented it to try to extract all the bad smells
our power station was creating. It never worked,
and I told Dr Pfooflepfeffer to throw it in the
skip. It looks like she just kept it! Look at the
waste being pumped out! It looks like . . . '

High above our heroes stood the imposing
exterior of Wilbur's wonky slime factory . . .

'POOOH!' said Rubi.

Dennis wasn't sure whether she was describing the brown gloopy sludge shooting up towards Fartmoor, or simply reacting to the exceptionally pongy niff in the chamber. The professor chuckled.

'The funny thing is, it will never work underground. Slime reacts most efficiently to *natural sunlight*. Maybe it would be possible today with improved solar-harnessing technology but back then . . . it was just too dirty and smelly to ever be worth developing properly.'

'Then all of this has been for . . . nothing?!' asked Sketch.

'Less than nothing!' laughed Rubi.

Professor Von Screwtop did the science bit. 'Natural sunlight heats the slime gently, extracting energy without releasing any harmful gases, just fresh air.'

'Artificial light causes a violent reaction in the slime, and it releases more harmful gases than energy. The light down here is all artificial, so this place can only generate a tiny amount of energy! It probably costs Wilbur more to run it than he'll ever make back.'

He looked sad. 'When we were developing this technology, the solar collectors available to us just weren't very good. Maybe with the panels we have today, you could . . .'

The professor looked thoughtful. He dug in his pockets for a pencil and a piece of paper, then began to began to scribble furiously.

IF I UPGRADE THE COLLECTOR, POLISH THE CHAMBER, SPRAY THE PUMP YELLOW AND CARRY THE ONE... THEN MAYBE, JUST MAYBE...

'So much for Dr P. being a science guru,' smirked Dennis. 'She's doing it all wrong.'

'She's very smart,' said the professor,

brandishing the piece of paper he'd been scribbling on. 'Her problem is likely that Wilbur wants to keep the process a secret – that's probably why this is all underground. I think if he just built the power plant in the open air, using new solar panels, it would probably work! To release energy, the slime must come into contact with Fission Chips and light. Then it releases energy and gas. It has to let the gas go somehow, so it shapes itself into as many bottoms as it needs to release it.'

'A butt chain reaction? Did I hear you right, Dad?' asked Rubi. 'Are you telling me the slime tries to create butts for itself so gas can escape?'

Prof Screwtop was delighted his precious

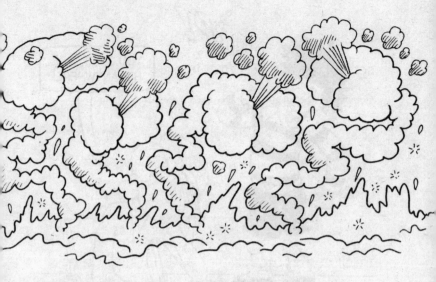

daughter was smarter than he'd been when he was ten.

'Exactly! Better out than in! It doesn't matter if the slime is pumping out fresh air or stinky farts: if you want to get rid of gases, then butts are best!'

'What about burps?' asked Dennis. 'Why fart and waste it when you can burp then taste it?!'

Rubi felt grossed out. Sketch ignored

Dennis and asked the professor how this could

possibly explain a slime monster chasing them

across Fartmoor?

'I think this happened because they are

using artificial light. Instead of the gentle release of energy that you get with natural light, the slime's reaction is too violent. It becomes hyper-energised and it needs to get rid of that energy quickly. It's a bit like a little kid who's eaten too many sweets and can't settle down. It gets mischievous and naughty and then maybe a bit angry, and before you know it, it it's been sent to its bed without any supper!'

Rubi took over. 'If everything is done correctly the process harvests the cleanest electricity the world has ever known. The only waste is fresh air. If it's done badly, you get hardly any energy and a whole lot of toxic waste. Simples.'

Only Rubi could describe this as simple.

By now, the scientific talk was boring Dennis, even the bit celebrating farts as an energy source. He was eyeing up the brightly lit control panel, hoping to discover a switch that would raise them all back to the surface so that he could get Gnasher to a good vet.

Bang in the centre was a large red button with a label that said:

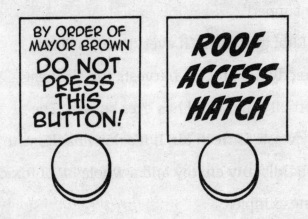

There was another button next to it:

ROOF ACCESS HATCH

RED BUTTONS ALWAYS DO GOOD THINGS, RIGHT?

Dennis pressed the first button. High above them, a beam of light blazed onto a mirror and was reflected straight down to the tank of slime below.

PHIZZZOGGGG!

The slime crackled with energy and began to expand within the confines of the glass dome. It fizzed like a warm diet cola bottle with chewy mints dropped in, and unleashed a chorus of pumps that grew in volume as they grew in volume*. The dials on the control panel showed that electricity production was at 0.1% and waste production at 99.9%!

> *Just a little science joke there! You see, the pumps get louder as they get bigger. Volume can mean how loud something is, or how much space something is occupying! Geddit? – The Ed, feeling very pleased with himself.

Then came a loud sound that reminded Dennis of the noise he made when finishing off the last drops of a thick milkshake. The brown waste was being sucked from the bottom of the tank and sent up a pipe that sprayed it into the air above ground, straight onto Fartmoor.

SCHLUUUUUURP!

Dennis hit the other button. Just because it was there, really.

There was a grinding noise from above. The roof was opening! As more and more light poured into the chamber, the slime bubbled more and more furiously.

Dennis jumped down to the ground, where his friends were more interested in what was happening to Gnasher. He was sparking quite furiously in the light.

'I've seen him bark furiously loads of times, but this is the first time ever for sparking furiously,' admitted Dennis.

MY SPARK IS WORSE THAN MY BITE!

'Quite remarkable,' said the professor, using a pocket-sized scanner to take some measurements. 'Your dog seems to be more reactive than the slime itself. It's like he's feasted on my Fission Chips. Not that there is any possibility of that, obviously . . .'

Sketch and Dennis looked down at the ground. They knew Gnasher had hungrily licked up the spilled Embarrassium during the er . . . eventful field trip at the Research Centre, and then he'd sampled the slime on the moor too. Even Dennis could do the maths. Inside Gnasher was a combination of Fission Chips and slime, and the light had just activated it.

Gnasher was filling up with gas! But, because of the fart pills Gnasher had taken, he was unable to pump it out! He was growing

bigger and bigger. Unless Dennis did something soon, his best friend would burst!

Rubi was far better at maths than Dennis, so she'd already worked out the problem they faced was even bigger than a humungous Gnasher.

'The slime on the surface will be reacting with the sunlight and Fission Chips. It's going to lead to an uncontrolled butt reaction. But outside the Sux-Capacitor, there's no way to control it. Slime could continue growing and destroy the whole town!'

'We are in great danger. The whole of Beanotown is! Our only chance is to try to draw the slime away from the surface.'

'Draw it away?'

Rubi turned and looked at Sketch.

ER, WHY ARE YOU LOOKING AT ME?

Chapter Twelve

BACK TO THE DRAWING BOARD!

Sketch rapidly illustrated Rubi's 'suck it and see' plan to make the waste pumps churning toxic slime out onto Fartmoor do the ultimate switcheroo and instead suck the waste back in!

If it worked, they'd clean Fartmoor, plus refill the hole created by the Mayor's secret power plant. Result!

'Wow! Wait until you get a load of this, guys!' said Sketch proudly.

They looked closely at what she had drawn and realised that Wilbur just couldn't help

himself. His logo was everywhere, not just on the skips, bin and binbags, but in the basic structure of his power station!

The supports that held the entire place up were shaped like a gigantic W. Sketch's drawing made it clear what they needed to do!

'You're a genius, Sketch,' said Rubi. All we have to do is fill a giant W-shaped swimming pool with toxic slime and keep it away from the light!'

Professor Von Screwtop explained the plan would only succeed if they worked together as a team. He described the three stages.

'First, turning the dillydoowhack off releases the electromagnet on the roof hatch, ensuring sunlight will flood in, activating the slime as its gasses expand.'

'I'll do that part,' offered Sketch.

'Next, twanging the whatsit at the same time will create a vacuum, meaning the toxic waste from Fartmoor will be sucked into Wilbur's dirty power plant. How perfect!'

'That's MINE,' demanded Rubi.

'Finally, twisting the thingummyjig will open the hatch on the side of the Sux-Capacitor so Gnasher can sneeze into the slime. One sneeze will introduce enough Fission Chips to begin the full butt reaction.'

Dennis volunteered. 'Simples! We'll take care of that. Right, Gnasher!'

'Are we ready to do this?' asked Rubi.

'One for all and all for fun!' yelled Sketch, and they took up their positions.

They all looked at each other, then turned, twanged, and twisted . . . but nothing happened.

'Uh?' said Dennis, certain he'd heard a loud twang.

FOR SNEEZE A JOLLY GOOD FELLOW . . .

162

An evil laugh echoed around the chamber. It was Dr Pfooflepfeffer clutching what looked like a tiny flying saucer.

'My dillydoowhackthingummyjigwhotsit remote control has allowed me to wreck your pathetic plan with one finger,' she cackled. Pfofflepfeffer stabbed the button again and more sparks flew!

Professor Von Screwtop yelled, 'Stop! You're agitating the molecules. Gnasher has just sneezed Fission Chips into the slime. You're awakening big trouble!'

'Blah! Blah! Blah! I really don't care,' replied Pfooflepfeffer as she tapped

OVERRIDE

the button repeatedly, opening the hatch then slamming it shut in quick succession.

The sunlight from outside flashed on and off, exciting the slime.

Sinister shapes began to form in the slime, and move ominously towards them. Like slime . . . zombies . . .

'Slimebies!' warned Professor Von Screwtop. 'Don't let them dribble on you, or you'll be turned into one of them!'

The slimebies started to slip and slide out of the safety hatch that Dennis had twisted open before Gnasher sneezed into it, like an army of slimy soldiers marching into battle. They homed in on the closest target: Dennis.

They slip-slopped towards him, farting and squelching so loudly that the warning screams

from his friends were drowned out. Was this
how it was all going to end for the world's
wildest boy? Fart-slimed into oblivion?!

Professor Von Screwtop appealed to Dr Pfooflepfeffer. 'Activate the whatsit. It's our only hope – only the mass influx of external slime can save Dennis now!'

'I'm sorry, but it appears I'm losing control!' smirked Pfooflepfeffer. She tossed the control into the middle of the slime, meaning there

was no escape. As Dennis watched it slip beneath the surface, he felt his hopes sink with it. Pfooflepfeffer turned and walked towards the desk to retrieve her smartphone.

'I'm going to film this as *scientific research*,' she said.

Dennis groaned. He didn't want millions of people watching him turn into a giant slimy bogey.

But, at this moment, he discovered that the only thing better than having a dog like Gnasher was having the supersized version! His paw-some size allowed him to leap over the advancing slimebie army, grab Dennis gently between his teeth and toss him over his head, onto his back. Dennis grabbed a handful of fur in both hands and hung on for dear life.

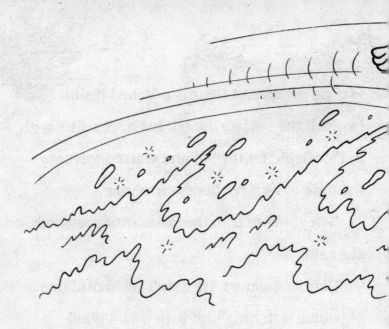

Gnasher stood on his hind legs and reached as high as he could, up to the platform where the dillydoowhack was situated. Dennis was able to climb up Gnasher's back to grab it.

Gnasher scrabbled with his paws against the platform, trying to get up to safety. Dennis pulled as hard as he could but it was an impossible task. The farting, snarling slime army was closing in . . .

Dennis suddenly had a scientific brainwave. Gnasher was so large because he couldn't release the gas inside of him. He couldn't fart, due to Gran's imported pills . . . but what if there was another way?

He put his hands on top of a massive paw and gently said what could well be his final words to his best mate.

'Gnash, I need you to let rip the biggest

burp of your entire life. Right now. Let it go!'

Gnasher looked confused, but then nodded and wagged his tail furiously.

BUUUUUUUUUUUUU

A rush of hot, sausage-scented air made Dennis's hair stand on end!

It was the most epic burp of all time. As the burple-coloured gas gushed out, Gnasher deflated back to his regular size, allowing Dennis to lift him to safety, in the nick of time! Gnasher helped Dennis twist the whatsit, closing the flap and preventing any more slime from escaping. Rubi shut down the thingummyjig and Sketch took care of the dillydoowhack.

A huge whooshing noise told them their

plan had worked! Inrushing toxic slime
from Fartmoor was being diverted safely
into the huge underground pits Sketch had
discovered in Wilbur's 'W' shape. The other
noise they heard was a shriek of rage from
Dr Pfooflepfeffer. Result!

The whole place shuddered, fell silent . . .
then went completely and utterly pitch black!

Chapter Thirteen

UNLUCKY FOR SOMEONE ELSE!

Dennis had never feared the dark, but this was spookier than a graveyard on Halloween.

Everyone nervously held their breath, waiting for whatever was about to happen next. Had their daring plan been a success, or were they about to be swamped by slime?

The silence was broken by a slight hiss, before the lights started to flicker and then, with a low electrical hum, glowed brighter than ever before.

The pipes shook, groaned and then began to

pump slime back into the pool, where it bubbled and boiled away, shrinking all the while.

'It worked!' cried Dennis.

Soon the slime was almost gone. Professor Von Screwtop scooped up the last of it in a test tube and popped it in his pocket. The pool was empty, save for a very yucky-looking remote control and a pair of broken glasses.

Dr Pfooflepfeffer was furious.

'What have you done?' she yelled furiously at the professor.

'A far better thing for science than you could ever imagine,' replied the prof. 'It's time for this experiment to wait until a greater brain is ready to work upon it. Like my daughter, Rubidium. One day she will finish my Fission Chips.'

ME? EVEN SMARTER THAN MY DAD?! WOW!

'I don't think so. By then, the planet will already be battered!' Dr Pfooflefeffer guffawed at her own evil genius. She laughed so hard that the kind Professor Von Screwtop rushed over to see if she was OK. He wanted to be sure she wasn't choking.

Instead, she swooped towards him and plucked the test tube from his pocket, like a seagull stealing a sandwich from a picnic on Beanotown beach. She leapt into the golf buggy and sped away, cackling as if she'd just pulled off the greatest prank in the planet's history. If they didn't get that test tube back, it would be the last prank in history.

Professor Von Screwtop was, for the third time in a day, in a crumpled heap upon the ground, wondering whatever had just happened to him. The only difference this time was that Rubi was angrier – far angrier.

Rubi had developed several enhancements for her chair, as a challenge to herself. She never really used them though as she didn't want to put other kids at an unfair disadvantage. She reckoned she'd give even Billy Whizz* a run for his money in the sprint at school sports day if she ever chose to activate her booster jets!

This was a different situation, however. She was up against a cunning grown-up, who'd just cruelly toppled her dad. Everything was fair game now. It was not only time for her to say game on, but also jets on!

* The fastest boy in the world.

Rubi's wheels spun, then screeched as she sped after Pfooflepfeffer, leaving behind a trail of burning rubber!

'Be careful, Rubi!' shouted Prof Von Screwtop as his daughter disappeared into the distance, already gaining on her target.

'After her!' cried Dennis. Gnasher, Sketch and Professor Von Screwtop followed Rubi on foot, knowing the fleeing Pfooflepfeffer would at least lead them safely out of Wilbur's underground lair.

Rubi was gaining quickly on Dr Pfooflepfeffer. A golf buggy was no match for her super charged chair. As she drew level she smiled over at Dr Pfooflepfeffer.

'Pull over, doc!'

'Silly girl! I'd never wear a pullover. This is

an expensive designer suit, the type you'll never be able to afford!'

Dr Pfooflepfeffer accelerated and drew away from Rubi, then cunningly unleashed some golf balls that had been left in the buggy. They bounced up and spun back towards Rubi, forcing her to take last-second evasive action to dodge them.

The doctor cackled as Rubi dropped farther back. As she did so, she flipped up a panel on at the side of her chair. It was time to play dirty. On the panel were three buttons, each of which activated a special feature, designed by Rubi after watching some secret-agent movies.

They first released a stream of golden syrup, which even the slipperiest customer couldn't wade through!

The second fired Super Strong Silly String, a speciality from Har-Hars' Joke Shop. Harsha in Class 2B had swapped some for Rubi's new 'Eggs-cellent' stink bomb formula. Rubi thought about how the string would ruin Dr Pfooflepfeffer's prized designer jacket. AWESOME!

Rubi noticed they were starting to climb a ramp. Ahead of them was a rocky wall, but Dr Pfooflepfeffer seemed to be speeding up. A strange sound was drifting back toward her too. The doctor was making weird noises. She was clucking like a chicken! She was daring Rubi to smash straight into wall ahead! When anyone dared Rubi to do anything, she did it, so Pfooflepfeffer had just made an epic error! Rubi accelerated straight into the wall, forgetting all the reasons she shouldn't. Her instinct was ordering her to do so.

COME AND HAVE A GO IF YOU THINK YOU'RE HARD ENOUGH!

She felt a breeze on her face as she emerged into the open air. The wall had actually been a clever hologram. Hologram technology –

the art of fake news – was her adversary's specialty! Rubi gulped in the fresh air. The nasty niff must've disappeared thanks to their plan. Pfooflepfeffer was zooming across Fartmoor back toward town. Rubi activated her ALL-TERRAIN TYRES and started to close the gap.

She saw the shock and bewilderment on Pfooflepfeffer's face as she drew closer again. She clearly hadn't bargained on Rubi's determination to catch her!

Rubi made a decision. She activated button three: her brand new wheel spikes. She'd kept this function secret from her dad and she'd always thought of them as more of a bling thing, but . . . needs must!

WHIRRRRRRRRRRR!

Shiny spikes emerged from the middle of Rubi's wheels. She drew up alongside Dr Pfooflepfeffer's kart and swerved so one of the spikes punctured the kart's back tyre!

As the tyre deflated, Pfooflepfeffer wrestled with the steering wheel. The kart skidded wildly from one side of Gasworks Road to the other, until the punctured tyre clipped the kerb, flipping the kart onto its roof and hurling Pfofflepfeffer right through the wrought iron gates outside 'Tranquility', home to none other than Wilbur – and Walter – Brown!

Rubi slowed her chair and released button three. The spikes whirred back into the wheels. She took a deep breath and sent a message over Groupchat, and then Dennis, Sketch and Gnasher arrived in another Beanotown Golf

Course golf kart. Seconds later, JJ, Minnie and Pie Face arrived.

'The slime just disappeared!' panted Minnie. 'Probably all down to me! What have you been up to?'

Sketch said, 'Soz, Rubes. We'd have got here sooner, but we only discovered the secret holographic doorway after Dennis tried to climb the wall . . .'

I GUESS SHE WENT THAT–A–WAY!

Rubi smiled. 'Let's just say we've all done our bit, even my dad!'

Dennis pointed at the bent and twisted gates. 'Looks like the doc's holed up with her old buddy the Mayor. I think it's time we paid them a visit!'

Chapter Fourteen

THE SLIMEBUSTERS!

No one enjoys being disturbed when they're
relaxing in their dressing gown. The Brown
boys were no different.

They'd been relaxing in the study, drinking hot chocolate and playing backgammon, when an angry Dr Pfooflepfeffer had noisily arrived. Things were beginning to get very unpleasant when Dennis and his friends trooped in to join the party.

Wilbur's face was a mixture of shock and annoyance. His top lip displayed a most-wanted evil moustache via a combination of hot choc and melted marshmallows. It made him look quite different. *Even more ridiculous*, thought Dennis.

'Just what do you think you're doing? Trespassers will be prosecuted,' threatened Walter. Dennis didn't even know what prosecuted meant, but surely anything that had the word cute in it could never truly be a bad thing?

PEOPLE LIKE YOU ARE THE REASON PEOPLE LIKE US HAVE TO BUILD BIG WALLS!

Dennis noticed there was still a space on the wall for the head of the Abominable Snowmenace. If only Wilbur tried reading a bit more, he might solve the mystery of that creature's disappearance.

Rubi interrupted. It was technically rude,

but she forgave herself given the unusual circumstances they were in.

'Your slime is over, Wilbur. Your plan to make – yet another – fortune flogging dirty power to the people of Beanotown has gone under. You need to clean up the mess that you've made.'

'Who cares? Wilbur retorted. 'I'll find another way to take your money soon enough. Clean it up yourselves – it was all working tickety boo when I left . . .'

'How can you say such a thing?' asked Sketch. 'You put everyone's health in danger!'

'Quite easily. I just open my mouth and out it pops,' he replied smugly. Walter stood up and gave his father a polite round of applause.

Dennis butted in. 'OK, fair enough. We'll

clear it up. But don't complain if we accidentally on purpose make another type of mess in exchange, one you'll never be able to sweep underneath your woolly mammoth rug.'

SALE PRICE
£100000000

Wilbur and Walter both arched an eyebrow. Dennis had their full and undivided attention. 'I feel there's a risk of another shocking leak. This time to our friend I.P. Daley for a feature in the *Beanotown Gazette*. Sketch has drawings of everything we've witnessed today.'

Wilbur scoffed at the threat. 'I'm not a complete idiot, and you can't prove a thing.'

'Oh, really?' replied Dennis. 'Well, what part's missing?'

Sketch heard the Mayor gulp loudly. Rubi thought it was funny the way Wilbur suddenly looked less sure of himself, so she pressed home their advantage.

'I.P. might think your slimy behaviour is shocking enough for her to write another best-selling book about your crooked antics, so millions of children worldwide will end up laughing their heads off about how pathetic your plan was.'

'She wouldn't dare. I'll speak to her editor and have her fired!'

'Perfect! Kids love reading about evil baddies!' said Sketch.

Dennis made a final offer. 'It's too late to stop everyone finding out about your power plant, and people need to know about that. But you ARE going to clean up Fartmoor, pay for Rubi's dad to complete his work on the slime-powered electricity farm and give the people of Beanotown free electricity for life, OR ELSE!'

I LAUGH IN THE FACE OF EVERY MENACE I EVER MEET!

'Or what?' scoffed Wilbur.

'Yeah!' laughed Walter. 'Or WHAT?!'

Dennis smiled.

'Or we'll tell the Golf Club you stole one of their golf buggies – and we CAN prove that!'

Wilbur and Walter gulped, then nodded his head meekly.

They didn't mind if anyone realised they'd nearly caused an environmental catastrophe, but they couldn't bear the mockery of their fellow golf club members, where buggy theft was a banning offence.

Beanotown Gazette

He's IN the hole! Disgraced Mayor locked up for theft!

Dennis smiled and closed the bargain.
'When I make a mess, Mum makes me clean it
up all by myself. So we want to see you three
up there on Fartmoor getting your hands dirty.
No paying someone else to do it for you!'

Again, Walter and Wilbur could only nod.

Rubi added, 'Even better, Sketch has
designed you some very flattering outfits to
wear while you're working. Very stylish, I'm
sure you'll agree. Show them, Sketch!'

Sketch held up her tablet, which had a
picture of the
three pesky
polluters
in snazzy
uniforms.

'Meet the Slimebusters!' chuckled Dennis.

As they left the mayor's house, Dennis held up the test tube of slime they'd retrieved.

'Careful, Dennis!' said Rubi. 'You might spill some of that extremely stinky slime!'

But before anyone realised what he was doing, Dennis let a few blobs of slime fall on the marble doorstep. His friends realised at once what he'd done.

SMELL YA LATER, WILBUR...

And that's why, from that day to this and into the future for who knows how long, the Brown family are followed at every step by the unmistakable sound of tiny, slimy farts.

Result!

The SCIENCE of SLIME

by Rubidium Von Screwtop

1. There are over 900 species of slime in the world!

2. The sline in your nose is called <u>mucus</u> and, gross as it may seem, it protects us from germs and diseases by blocking dirt and bacteria.

<u>nose</u>

<u>nasties</u>

3. Slime is like social media for snails and slugs! They leave a trail as a way of communicating!

4. Vinegar completely dissolves slime!! Try it and see! I wish we'd known that earlier and we'd have headed straight to Beantown's Fish + Chip shop!

5. Playing with a handful of slime has been proven to relieve stress!

6. Some creatures produce slime to distract predators!

Hagfish use it to choke other fish who attack! (it's rEELy effective - LOL!)

7. A fear of slime is called "Blennophobia"

8. The furthest a piece of slime has been stretched is 224 cm in 30 seconds!

Beat that!!

Thanks Rubi! -DENNIS

About the Authors

Craig Graham and Mike Stirling were both born in
Kirkcaldy, Fife, in the same vintage year when Dennis
first became the cover star of Beano. Ever since,
they've been training to become the Brains Behind
Beano Books (which is mostly making cool stuff for
kids from words and funny pictures). They've both
been Beano Editors, but now Craig is Managing Editor
and Mike is Editorial Director (ooh, fancy!) at Beano
Studios. In the evenings they work for I.P. Daley
at her Boomix factory, where Craig fetches coffee
and doughnuts, and Mike hoses down her personal
bathroom once an hour (at least). It's the ultimate
Beano mission!

Craig lives in Fife with his wife Laura and
amazing kids Daisy and Jude. He studied English so
this book is smarter than it looks (just like him).
Craig is partially sighted, so he bumps into things
quite a lot. He couldn't be happier, although fewer
bruises would be a bonus.

Mike is an International Ambassador for
Dundee (where Beano started!) and he lives in
Carnoustie, famous for its legendary golf course.
Mike has only ever played crazy golf. At home, Mike
and his wife Sam relax by untangling the hair of
their adorable kids, Jessie and Elliott.